# It's a Moose!

★

## MEG ROSOFF
## DAVID ERCOLINI

putnam

G. P. PUTNAM'S SONS

**For Ben and Anika —M. R.**

**For Ella, Ellis, Scarlett, and Rosie —D. E.**

G. P. PUTNAM'S SONS

An imprint of Penguin Random House LLC, New York

Text copyright © 2020 by Meg Rosoff

Illustrations copyright © 2020 by David Ercolini

G. P. Putnam's Sons is a registered trademark of Penguin Random House LLC.

Visit us online at penguinrandomhouse.com

Library of Congress Cataloging-in-Publication Data ✧ Names: Rosoff, Meg, 1956– author. | Ercolini, David, illustrator. ✧ Title: It's a moose! / Meg Rosoff; illustrated by David Ercolini. ✧ Other titles: It is a moose! ✧ Description: First edition. | New York, NY: G. P. Putnam's Sons, [2020] ✧ Summary: A baby that is different from all the others brings a family great joy until he grows too big for their home. ✧ Identifiers: LCCN 2016021492 | ISBN 9780399166648 (hardcover) ✧ Subjects: | CYAC: Babies—Fiction. | Moose—Fiction. | Animals—Infancy—Fiction. ✧ Classification: LCC PZ7.R719563 It 2020 | DDC [E]—dc23 ✧ LC record available at https://lccn.loc.gov/2016021492

Manufactured in China

ISBN 9780399166648

10 9 8 7 6 5 4 3 2 1

Design by Dave Kopka and Suki Boynton

Text set in Verlag

The art was done in tempera paint on paper and Photoshop.

When our new baby arrived, he had velvety soft skin and big brown eyes. He ate twigs and weeds.

We were all expecting the usual sort of baby, so imagine our surprise. Instead of feet, he had four perfect hooves. And his nose!

I felt sad for the other babies. They all looked the same.

We couldn't wait to take him home and dress him in little suits.

Grandma said he is the spitting image of her great-aunt Lydia.

Our baby has very long legs.

We can hang things on his antlers.

His ears are silky.

We would not trade him for anything.
He is the world's most beautiful baby.

Whenever we take him out,
strangers stop to admire his lovely eyes.
They point at him from across the street and stare.
They wish they had a baby like ours.

One day I took him to school for show-and-tell, and everyone wanted to peek. Is it an eyeball? A rat? A shoe? Not one person guessed.

All my friends wanted
a moose baby.

Our baby grew so fast. Soon he was big and strong, and could run as fast as a bus.

Then he was bigger than Dad.
We had to take him places in
a special car.

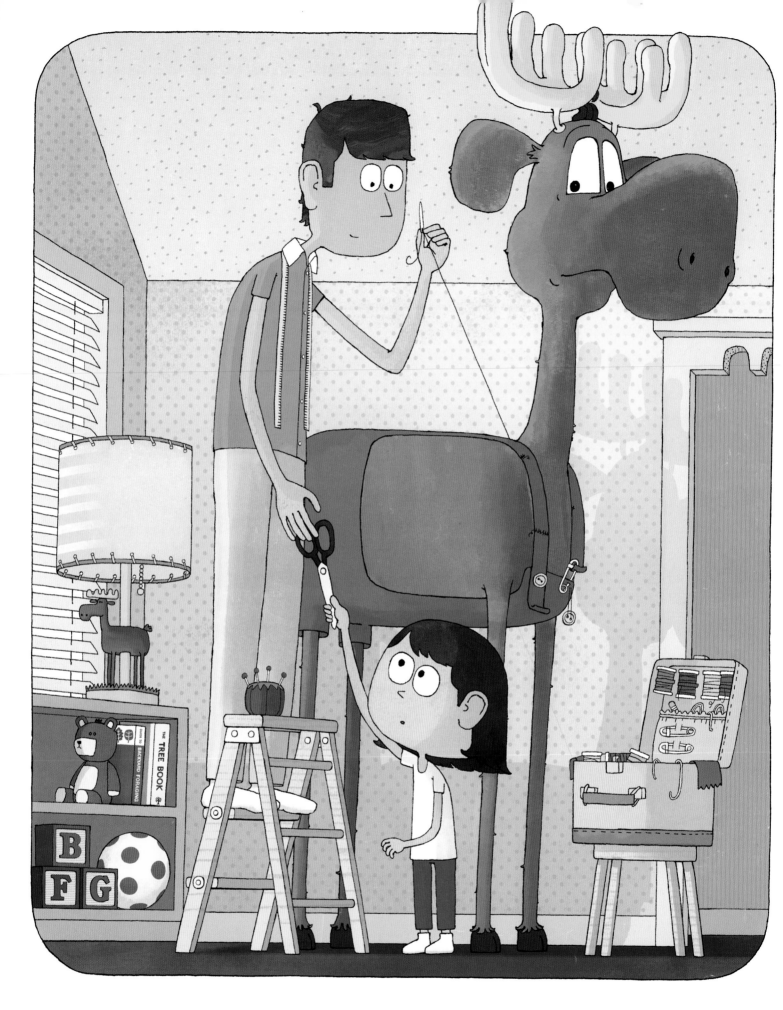

None of his new clothes fit.

Everything seemed too small.

The house seemed too small.
We seemed too small, too.

Night after night, our baby stayed in his room and sang. Some of his songs seemed sad. There was only one thing to do.

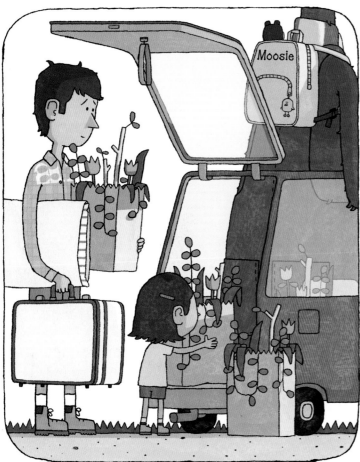

We packed his bags. And put on his traveling goggles.
We filled the car with provisions, studied the map, and set off.

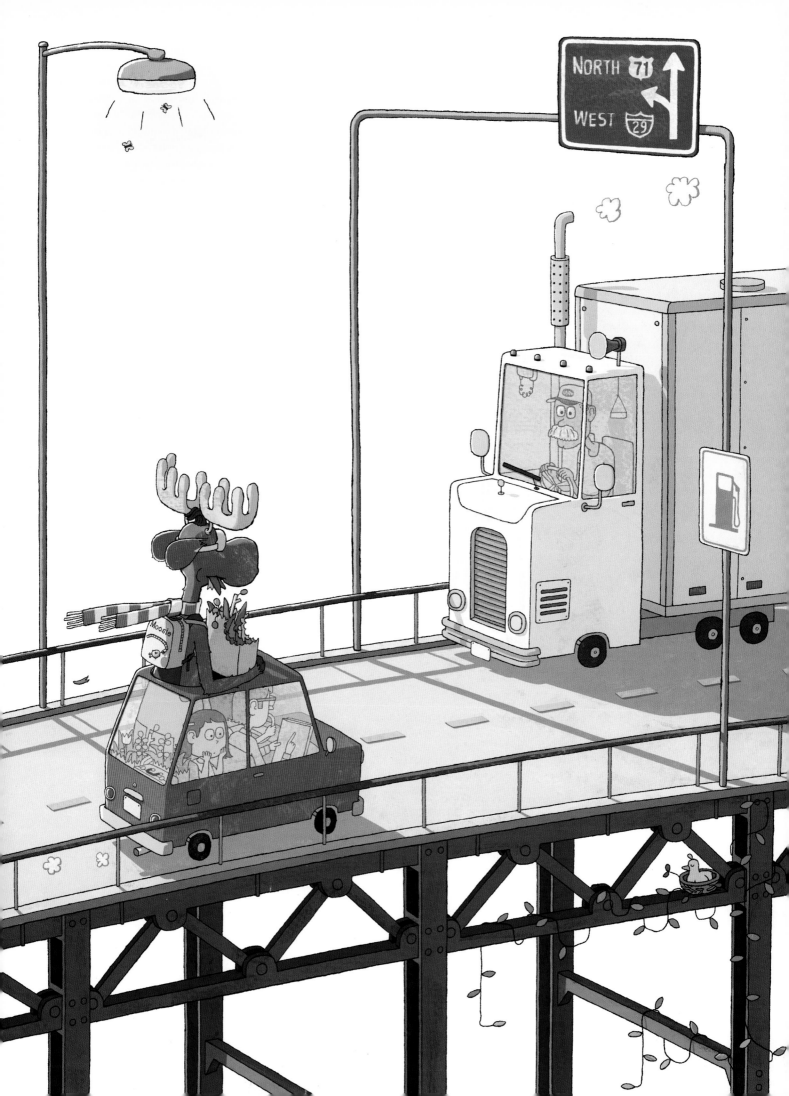

We drove. And drove. And drove. And drove. And drove.

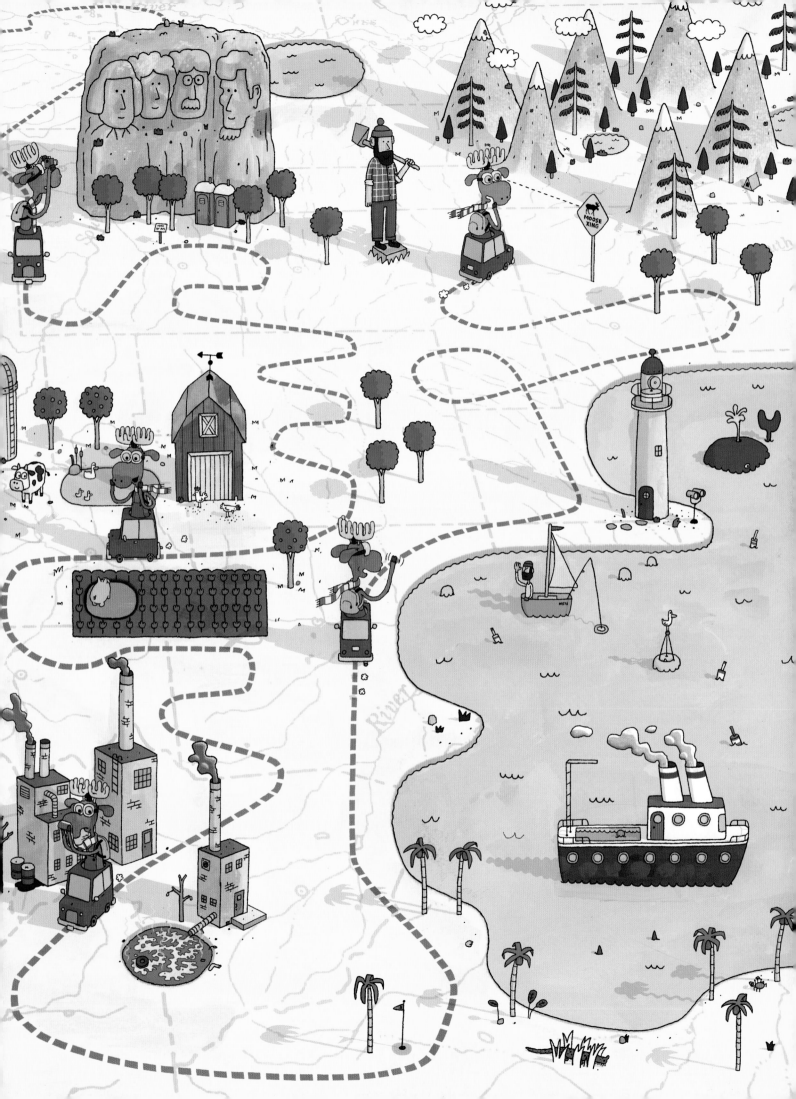

When we reached the mountains, our baby looked surprised. He sniffed the pine trees. He sniffed the clean air. He sniffed the twigs and weeds and the birds in the trees and the fish in the stream.

He tasted the new place.

He sang a new song and
it wasn't sad.

He met another moose baby and they played together.

At last it was time to say goodbye.

Our baby looked back at us for
a minute, but then he was off.
"Don't forget to write," we called,
but did he remember to pack a pen?

A week later we got a postcard.

Here's what it said: